CW00865964

Story, text and cover design by Damian Powell

Condition of sale:
This book is sold subject to the condition that it shall not,
by way of trade or otherwise, be lent, hired out or
otherwise circulated without the publisher or authors
prior written consent in any form of binding or cover
other than that in which it is published and without a
similar condition including this condition being imposed
on the subsequent purchaser. No part of this publication
may be reproduced, stored in a retrieval system or
transmitted in any form or by any means without the
prior written permission of the publisher or author
Damian Powell

© 2016 Damian Powell

For further information please visit:
www.damianpowell.co.uk

Foreword

By Dr. Paul McCormac Clinical Psychologist

I've known Damian for as long as I can remember - my memories of Damian go back to burying each other in the biggest sandpit ever in his back garden and exploring the small wooded area behind the back of the house he grew up in. The Jungle, as it was known to all the neighbourhood kids, was a place for imaginations to run wild. I also remember a garden full of chickens and rabbits and camping trips to his family farm. Damian has an unending capacity to see the lighter side of life and I don't think we had a serious conversation for 20 of those 40+ years. Yet he has a capacity to say what needs to be said at the right time and in the right quantity that I've always admired. My Mate Damian the Magician has worked some of this magic of his into his book.

My Dad the Magician gently encourages us to think about the inevitable finality of life and to contemplate how we might engage in conversations with those to whom the losses matter the most. I can envisage My Dad being used to initiate those conversations with a necessary gentleness and playfulness without skirting around a confronting issue.

In my own work as a Clinical Psychologist I often see the suffering that people of any age can be left with when there is an unexplained loss where there has been no preparation or planning. This book would make an invaluable resource to parents and children to begin those seemingly impossible conversations.

Readers of My Dad will be reminded of the priceless value of the relationships we might hope to have with our children. You will be reminded of the importance of making the most of being available to children with whatever time we hope we have to give them. You will also be encouraged to think about the true value of that time poured into those relationships with children in preparing them for their losses and grief.

If you are contemplating your own conversations with children about loss and grief or know of someone who is I don't think you could go far wrong in using or recommending My Dad the Magician as a place to start that journey.

Dr. Paul McCormac
Clinical Psychologist
B.Sc. (Hons), D.Clin. Psych.,
Member of the Australian Psychological Society
Member of the Australian College of Clinical Psychologists

My Dad the Magician

Chapter 1

It was steak night, and Eric Jones loved steak.

There were chips, peas, mushrooms fried in butter, battered onion rings, tomato relish and not forgetting a plate filling, juicy, fat, well-cooked steak, slightly crispy around the edges but soft and red in the middle.

Eric licked his lips, then downed half a glass of diet coke and let out a massive "aaaaahhhh" to show his appreciation to the chef, Dad.

'Perfect' he said, 'Thanks, Dad'

After the main event and some super tasty sticky toffee pudding that went down ever so well, Mum cleared up and loaded the dishwasher. Dad sat still, earning his ten-minutes rest for cooking the greatest meal on the planet, ever.

Kate, his older sister, and ever headphone wearing teenager sloped away with a doomed teenager look on her face that no one could tell if she was either extremely happy or miserably sad.

She didn't speak, she just left. She might have liked the steak, she might have loved it, but there was no way of knowing, just a tinny headphone sound leaving the room.

Eric and Dad just sat at the table, both looking very content with the feast they had just eaten.

'What's brown and sticky?' Eric blurted out.

Dad laughed before the question was finished, 'Get some new jokes son' he said, 'that's old, why are pirates called pirates? Because they aaaaaah!'

Eric just stared back, the look that says 'if you're not laughing at mine I'm sure not going to laugh at yours'

They stared at each other for forty-five seconds before Eric gave in and started giggling. 'Come here' said Dad, and Eric climbed over the table to give his Dad the biggest of hugs.

"Love you", "love you more", "love you mostest"

"Right then, homework!" Mum shouted through from the kitchen "let's get up them stairs"

"Duh" came the reply from the dining room.

"Go on lad, I'll put you to bed once you're done, maybe catch a few YouTube videos before you fall asleep"

Eric kissed his Dad, one more massive hug then ran upstairs to start his homework with Mum.

Dad coughed loudly and stayed sat at the table staring at his fingernails, before giving a quick head turn and a huge smile as Eric bounced his way upstairs.

Chapter 2

"He's waiting for you!" Mum shouted down as she disappeared into the bathroom for her well needed one hour luxury soak.

Dad grabbed his phone and skipped up the stairs to finish his day in his favourite way. It was story and YouTube time.

If there's one thing Eric loves its Dad and him sharing a phone screen under the covers in his bed watching some funny clip about cats, dogs or adventurous slip ups.

As if by clockwork one hour later Mum came in and had to drag Dad out of bed, both of them fast asleep, the light still on, the washing up piled high downstairs, the dog not walked and no cup of tea for Mum.

It was the same every night, but Mum knew how important this time together was for them both. She laughed to herself as Dad finally got himself together and plodded downstairs muttering under his breath about dishes, jobs and things.

6.45 am, it was Thursday morning and Eric was up and on Mum and Dads bed, "Come on Dad, come on Mum"

"Let's get up, let's do something!" he says.

It was July 25th and Eric was four days into his summer holiday. The word excited didn't even start to describe the way he felt, he knew Dad was off from now until next Tuesday, so he had to make the most of every minute.

Mum rolled over, she knew it was Dad that Eric wanted most and gave a gentle push on Dads body to get him out of bed.

"Ok, ok" said Dad, "not so fast young man, some of us need time to wake up" Dad stood up, then sat down again, and finally stood straight holding Eric's hand, and walked out towards the bathroom where he vanished for five minutes whilst Eric sat on the top step of the stairs waiting.

He heard Dad coughing, and finally a flush, then Dad came out looking just as bedraggled as before.

"Come on then tiger, let's get some brekky" he says.

Dad got organised in the kitchen, Eric let the dog out and dragged the two garden chairs from the conservatory so they could eat outside. They sat quietly together before discussing their plan for the day, which Dad played down by saying they should just hang around the house and watch films, but there was no tricking Eric, he knew today was fairground day and nothing was going to stop that.

Eric noticed Dad coughing again, and pushed the glass of water over to him, which he drank in one magnificent gulp.
9 am. Off they went, the fairground opened at 9.30 and they were only a 10-minute drive away. Just Eric and Dad all day, he could hardly contain his excitement.

Dad was his bestest friend ever in the whole great big wide universe and he told him again and again and again. This day was a good one.

Chapter 3

On Friday morning Dad's sister came over.

She arrived super early as Mum and Dad were going out for the day. No one told Eric where, so he presumed a shopping trip somewhere.

''I hope they buy me something'' he thought to himself.

Eric really liked his Aunt Sue, she was a lot of fun and always had a fantastic surprise for him.

Today she had decided they would start with an early morning cinema trip, followed by Pizza then to the beach with her two mad dogs Bouncer and Jack.

''Brilliant'' said Eric, smiling.

Eric said bye to Mum and Dad, gave Mum a big hug and Dad an even bigger one.

Dad held him right back and kissed the top of his head, then turned away sharply to stare out of the window, tears filled his eyes and his voice wobbled as he said 'Goodbye'' again to Eric as he ran off to his Aunt.

Today wasn't a good day for Dad.

Chapter 4

That evening was a weird one for Eric.

Eric and his Aunt Sue had come home at 6 pm as expected, hoping to see shopping bags and gifts and get his hugs and kisses from Mum and Dad, but instead there was a quietness filling the house.

Mum and Dad were in, they were upstairs.

His sister was in the kitchen plugged into her music. Eric looked up at his Aunt and saw her face change from super happy and full of fun to a saddened thoughtful one. Something was obvious to her how Mum and Dad's day had turned out.

Eric ran upstairs and was met by his Mum standing in the bedroom doorway, trying to close it but not quite managing due to a loose black shoe on the floor.

"Dad's just having a shower honey", she said "He'll be out soon"

He wasn't. Eric could just see his Dad through the crack in the doorway, curled up on the bed, but he didn't say anything.

He was a good boy and just did what Mum and Dad said. So off to his room he went and waited.

He lay with his eyes open for what seemed like forever. In fact, he waited so long that he eventually fell asleep, unaware of the conversations and tears going on downstairs.

Chapter 5

"Hey son" said Dad "what are you doing lying in all your clothes from yesterday?"

Eric looked down and laughed, "I don't know" he replied.

It was seven o'clock in the morning.

The joy of being only seven years old was that Eric had little memory of last night's weirdness. Today was a new day, today was a day with Dad again.

"What we doing then Dad?" he asked "can we go to the canal?"

"Course we can, let's get changed and get out early before anyone else wakes up" said Dad.

Off they set, out of the house by 7.45 and off for yet another adventure. The canals and the locks were one of Eric's favourite visits. He loved the boats going up and down, seeing the people on them living a much different life.

He loved the fact that it was just him and Dad and at some time they would settle into a massive pub lunch.

Dad was being super way more than ever friendly today, buying anything Eric asked for, and doing whatever Eric wanted.

This was usual but Eric noticed a slight change in Dad's normal constraints. He wasn't always this generous with his money.

They sat in the canal side pub after three hours of watching the boats. Dad ordered for them both and they sat by the large open bay window to see any other canal barges come and go.

Eric saw Dad staring into space so he threw a pea at him.

There was no response so he threw another. This time it caught Dad on the nose and he spun his head round in shock as if blasted by a water cannon.

"Sorry kiddo" said Dad "I was miles away"

He then turned his head to the window again and stared outside at the water passing by.

Eric knew something wasn't right. Dad looked so sad.

"Dad", Eric said, "are you ok, is something the matter?"

His Dad turned to him, it was obvious he was upset, he had a wet shine over his eyes.

"No, I'm fine son, just tired, I didn't sleep well last night, what's your food like?" followed by a massive fake yawn to show just how tired he was.

There was half a plate of food left on Eric's side of the table, Dad's was untouched.

"Yummy" he said "loved it, what's wrong with yours?"

Dad forced a chip into his mouth, laughed a little and said "I'm full"

Dad's eyes lowered to the table, and then slowly his head turned away again to look outside.

Eric just sat and stared at Dad unable to do anything to cheer him up.

He moved around the table and sat next to Dad and leant on him, followed by the words

"I love you Dad"

Eric didn't see it but Dad's face tightened up, he closed his eyes and held back a flood of tears, and somehow mumbled the words "You too sunshine."

Chapter 6

That night after Eric should have been asleep for hours he sat at the top of the stairs listening.

He knew Mum and Dad were talking about something important. He was hoping to hear but could only make out slight whispers from the living room.

His Aunt had been round again and his parents had said that he may see quite a bit of her over the next few months as she may be moving in for a while, to help out.

To help with what he didn't know.

Eric didn't like Dad being sad. Dad was always the happy one, the go-getter, the party starter, the one who made everyone else happy.

His Dad was the very best Dad in the whole wide world EVER.

His Dad was the one who took care of everyone else when they had problems, "so what was wrong with him now? Why was he so gloomy?" Eric thought.

Then he heard Dad coughing and moving about, the living room door opened so Eric ran back to bed without anyone seeing him.

He heard his Dad coughing, a lot, again.

Chapter 7

7.15 am the next morning, Eric bounced out of bed. The sun was shining, the birds were singing, he could hear Mum in the kitchen so he ran down.

"Hi Mum, where's Dad?" This was the usual welcome to Mum, all Eric ever wanted was his Dad.

"Oh, he's upstairs somewhere Hun, doing something, maybe in the show......" she didn't get to finish her sentence, Eric had turned and gone.

"Daaaaaaad", he shouted "Daaaaaaad – Oh!"

Dad was fast asleep in bed, curled up under the blankets, he looked dreadful.

So Eric woke him up.

"Come on, let's go out, let's play, let's do something exciting" Eric was shouting "Come on, wakey wakey"

Dad responded with a few grunts, pulled the covers back over him, he then went quiet again.

It was a trick. He then threw the covers off and jumped out of bed, weirdly followed by a swaying action that Eric hadn't seen before.

"Whoa!" said Dad. "That was close"

He steadied himself against the wall then slowly walked Eric back downstairs for breakfast, blaming an invisible piece of Lego on the floor for his wobble.

"Let's go shopping," said Dad, "let's go treat ourselves to some lovely things"

Mum said she was meeting friends so it just left Eric and Dad, best mates with a wallet full of cash and a free day.

"There's something I want to buy," said Dad "I have a plan."

Chapter 8

After two super boring clothes shops where Dad spent what felt like hours buying nothing, the two of them finally arrived at a small back street shop in a part of the town where Eric had never visited.

Above the shop was an old wooden sign that looked at least five hundred years old.

It read, ***"MISTER MANIONS' MAGICAL MYSTERY STORE"***

The door creaked and shook as it opened like it hadn't been moved in a century.

Dad's eyes widened as he stood in the doorway staring in. Shelves and cabinets were full of boxes of everything magical ever created.

Eric let go of Dad's hand and rushed in to get a closer look. Every spare bit of space had something in it, all mystical.

Boxes were labelled with names of tricks.

Eric liked the Disappearing Golden Rings and shouted "let's get this, no that one, no this one" as he ran around the store.

Another very squeaky door opened at the back of the shop.

An old man, who was very tall with a huge long white beard, appeared from a door at the back of the shop to welcome Eric and Dad.

His waistcoat was full of stars and rainbows. His tie was bright orange to match his pants, and the white shirt he wore had the baggiest arms Eric had ever seen.

Then he spoke in a weird voice that sounded to Eric like he came from another world altogether.

"Ah! Mr Jones. What a real pleasure to have you in my store" The shopkeeper bowed as he shook Dad's hand.

Eric looked at his Dad. How did this magical store keeper know who his Dad was, and why did he bow to him like that.

Dad said "Hello" back to the old man and gave a smile that said that they knew each other very well.

Eric was puzzled, and Dad knew that look on his face.

"This" Dad said "is Harry Manions, probably the second greatest magician to ever live"

"Second?" the old man replied, "Second... to whom?"

"To me of course" said Dad.

Eric was now really confused, was his Dad a magician?

Dad and the old magic shop keeper talked for five minutes or so while Eric checked out the shelves and boxes of tricks laid out in front of him. Eric kept looking back at Dad with a puzzled grin.

"So" said Dad, "I'm after buying something for my boy to start his love of magic, what have you got to blow his mind?"

Chapter 9

Dad and Eric sat outside the Derby Road cafe at a two seater table. The sun was hot, and lunch was on its way to them.

Eric only had eyes for the magic box on the table in front of him.

It was a shiny silver metal container, approximately ten centimetres wide, ten centimetres deep and three centimetres high.

The hinged lid was heavy and stiff. It was old, very old. It squeaked slightly when it was moved, and Dad promised to oil it later.

Inside the box was purple velvet lining the bottom and the walls and the inside of the lid.

It was empty except for dust, "probably from the days of the pyramids" Eric thought.

He felt inside again, definitely empty.

He closed the lid, tapped the top three times, repeated what Dad had taught him "Abracadabra" then counted to three.

On three he opened the lid slowly and there, yet again laid another shiny new fifty pence piece.

Eric was now two pounds and fifty pence up so continued to ask Dad to show him again, knowing how rich he would be by the end of the day.

He was amazed how it worked, but cunningly also knew how to milk it as long as possible until Dad ran out of change.

"It's just a trick" he thought to himself, "although it is clever."

"Who's the greatest magician ever kiddo?" asked Dad.

"I don't know" came the reply from Eric, "who? The old man in the shop?"

'I'll tell you" he said, and so Dad went back over the last two hundred years of magic history while Eric stared at him, intrigued by the tales of Houdini, Copperfield, Daniels and many other famous greats.

Dad told about the escapes from knife filled boxes, daring hanging manacled men fighting for their freedom over shark-infested pools of water,

Magical women appearing from empty boxes live on stage in theatres in London, and the tricks of the mind played to thousands of audiences on Saturday night television.

"However" said Dad. "And listen carefully. There is one trick that has a flaw. There is one huge amazing trick that no one has completely fulfilled."

Dad told Eric about the greatest magicians across the centuries enthralling audiences around the globe with their amazing disappearing tricks.

He told of Houdini, once named as the greatest magician in the world ever, who vanished in front of over one thousand people during a live show, only to reappear seconds later in another part of the theatre.

He told of 'Double M', the twins from Kansas who after being locked in a safe then chained and lowered into the water had shown up thirty seconds later outside the pool.

Finally, he told Eric about Mr Manions who in 1995 had been tied up, lowered in a coffin into the ground, and covered in soil had calmly reappeared thirty seconds later behind a church gravestone.

"You see Eric" Dad continued, "the greatest magician has an issue. He has a problem, a flaw in his trick. The best magician in the world would be the one who can not only pull off a show, can disappear from sight, but more importantly can disappear F O R E V E R. Now that would be real magic. No trace. No sign. Just gone...F O R E V E R"

"And" he continued leaning forward and whispering with a wink,

"I think I know how to do it"

Chapter 10

The next morning Eric and Mum sat eating breakfast, a bowl of honey cereal each, Mum with a cup of tea, Eric with a small glass of creamy milk.

Dad had been sick during the night and the house seemed very quiet while he caught up on some sleep upstairs.

"Should I take him a drink Mum?" asked Eric, "cheer him up?"

There was no answer so he asked again, but louder this time with a very caring tone to his voice. Mum shook her head and gave a slight smile just on one side of her mouth.

Eric knew that the plans they had made for today weren't going to happen now.

He had heard Dad three times during the night getting up and being ill in the bathroom, which was right next door to Eric's room.

He'd also heard Mum and Dad talking, a lot, about him being sick, and what they should do about it. Dad kept saying "shhh!"

"Is Dad ok Mum?" Eric asked, his Mum just nodded and carried on washing up.

Eric finished his cereal, put his bowl in the sink, kissed Mum and slumped away to the comfy red sofa in the living room.

The TV was on but he wasn't watching. He just wanted Dad to come down. His eyes kept looking up and towards the stairs. He wanted to go out and have fun with his Dad.

But Dad didn't come down that day, in fact, it wasn't until the next lunchtime that Dad finally made it downstairs.

"Sorry son" he said weakly "what do you want to do today? Let's do something quiet but fun"

Eric had a plan. One that would make him very happy and would keep Dad rested until he was better.

Chapter 11

In Eric's bedroom he had laid out some books, he had the magic box on his desk and the laptop was open with a paused video of Double M, the twins from Kansas who pulled off the biggest disappearing trick live on TV ever.

Dad sat on the bed looking around his son's room while Eric pulled up a chair to face him.

"Let's do some magic Dad" he said excitedly. "Can we learn some tricks, can you show me something?"

Dad's face lit up like someone had just turned a light on, the colour came back from pale white to somewhere a bit pinkish.

"Let's do it" Dad replied, "let's stay in here until we are amazing magical super mystical magicians. Or at least till lunchtime"

Eric laughed, Dad followed on too with a big giggle. "So what's that video on the laptop, let me see" asked Dad.

They watched 'Double M' together on the bed and Eric kept pausing trying to work out how the trick was done.

The scene was simple enough, the two identical brothers were tied together at the hands and feet, then large chains were placed around them, and they then climbed into a large bank safe, locked in then lowered into a pool of water.

Their four assistants were dressed in black clothes and black masks.

The clock started ticking, everyone knew the water was leaking into the safe.

Tick tock, tick tock.

One minute later an alarm went off which indicated that the safe was now full of water.

Tick tock, tick tock.

Eric looked at his Dad, his mouth slightly open.

Another minute later and another alarm went off. "How can they breathe?" asked Eric.

Dad shrugged his shoulders.

Finally, after three whole wet minutes, the safe was lifted from the pool, water poured out from every gap around the door. It was lowered onto the poolside and one of the assistants unfastened the safe door.

Eric gasped as the door opened. It was empty, nothing but drops of water.

Then with a loud bang, two of the assistants took off their masks. Amazingly it was the twins.

Eric stared at the screen, rewound the video a little to try and find out when they had got out, or if they hadn't even got in.

"its magic son" proclaimed Dad "Just magic"

"But" he continued "they all reappear, so it's not real magic, is it? If they were the greatest magicians in the world they would disappear FOREVER"

Chapter 12

Next morning Eric was sat upright in bed, he was listening to Dad, coughing in the bathroom again.

Not just coughing but real choking noises too. Mum had said to leave him alone, she said "Dad was just feeling a bit sick."

Eric sat, listened, and worried.

Then he cried.

Hearing Dad's pain saddened Eric a lot. He loved his Dad so much and needed him to be well again.

He checked his watch, Saturday 7.30 am.

Football lessons start at 10.30. "Would Dad be better" he thought.

Finally, after twenty minutes of shower noise and Dad trumping a lot and as loud as he could, a fresh-faced Dad came out of the bathroom, followed by a gazillion tonnes of steam.

"That's not all smoke from my trumps" Dad said.

"Ready to fight another day?" he followed on, as he paraded himself across the stairs and landing in his very short bright orange towel.

"Where's my favourite football player?" he said

"Here I am" Eric bounced back "Eric Beckham ready to play."

By 11 am two goals were down to Eric's skill, each one deserving a knowing nod from Dad.

Eric loved nothing more than scoring a goal and checking Dad's happy and proud face.

"Golden Arches?" asked Dad, their sign that McDonald's was this lunchtime's hangout.

"Brilliant" replied Eric "I am starving, I could eat a whole portion of fries with a burger and a drink and chicken pieces and ice cream on my own". He licked his lips.

Chapter 13

Sunday morning and Dad was in the bathroom again, coughing forever, followed by twenty minutes in the shower and some more serious trumping.

Breakfast that day was a quiet affair, not just because it was Sunday, but because Dad wasn't well, again. This time he looked really ill, pale, tired and just out of energy.

Eric stayed quiet, and stared a lot at Dad.

Every now and then Dad would lower his spoon as if it weighed the same as a bookcase.

Today wasn't a good day for the family.

Eric's auntie was on her way over, and Eric's sister had been "invited' to go and stay at Grandmas for a short while.

Dad asked Eric to set up the YouTube in his room, "Let's watch some magic Son, see if you can spot the faults in any tricks. I'm going to show everyone how this is done properly."

Three hours passed, they had a great time chatting, watching and laughing, however, Dad had fallen fast asleep on Eric's bed, so he left him there and went to head downstairs.

He heard Mum and his auntie chatting, so like any nosy seven-year-old he sat and tried to listen to what they were saying.

"It'd be better if he knew" he heard his Auntie saying, followed by Mums reply "No, we have a plan"

"Better if he knew? Plan? Knew what? What plan?" Eric, though. "What were they talking about?"

Eric went down, but by the time he got there his Mum and Auntie were talking about shopping and underwear, something Eric wanted to know nothing about.

"I'll be outside" he shouted.

He looked backed and knew they were talking about something again, something he wasn't supposed to hear.

Chapter 14

"Six weeks off! Where did that go?" thought Eric

The holidays were over, and typically today was roasting.

Brilliant sunshine and it was time to go back to school.

"Phuh" thought Eric "That didn't last long"

Everyone got up and got dressed, the house was quiet, no one seemed to be in a happy mood, and Mum didn't even take the new school year photos outside the house.

The car journey was silent for the whole ten-minute drive.

Both Mum and Dad came in with him that day, they said they had a very important appointment with the headmaster, Mr Jenkins.

Eric didn't ask, just in case it was about him. Whatever it was it didn't feel good in the car that day.

At the school gate, Eric stood with his parents, a few of his friends were running around kicking a ball.

Two of his girly classmates walked passed and said together "Good morning Eric Jones", he didn't reply and just pretended he was checking out his new shoes and hadn't noticed them.

The sun was beating down now, and Dad was getting uncomfortable in the heat and kept whispering something to Mum, before kissing Eric and going back to sit in the car.

"I'll come and get you in ten minutes" said Mum and slowly let go of his hand.

"Mum" said Eric, "What's actually wrong with Dad? Is he going to get better as he's been ill all holiday"

Almost with perfect timing, and to save Mum having to answer, Mr Jenkins came over to say hello.

"I'll be free as soon as the children have gone in" he said, "Should be about fifteen minutes"

Mum nodded, then turned to start chatting with a few other Mums, who all seemed to have a certain look on their faces. One was almost crying.

"Phuh" thought Eric "You'd think they'd be glad to send their kids back to school"

Finally, the school bell rang, Mr Jenkins came back to the steps, his sidekick Miss Jackson stood beside him as they ushered the children into the school starting with the year ones. Eric hugged his Mum, looked around to see if Dad was anywhere, kissed her and ran off with his friends up the school steps.

Mum took a tissue from her pocket and wiped her eyes, her friend to her left placed her hand on Mum's arm and put her head to one side.
"Time to tell school" she said, "I'd best go and get his Dad".

Chapter 15

3.30 pm It was home time and Dad was there to pick Eric up.

As usual, they had a massive hug and Dad smacked a huge kiss on Eric's forehead. He didn't mind at all, not even in front of his mates.

"Fish and Chips or Indian? What do you fancy?" asked Dad. "Tonight it's all your choice."

"Tonight we do exactly what you want. Mum's gone to see your Sister and Granny. It's just you and me kiddo"

Eric stared at an empty space behind Dad's head for three whole seconds before his response "Indian of course"

It was a perfect September evening as Dad and Eric walked the one-mile trek to the Temple of Raj Restaurant in their Village.

They held hands all the way, skipped for some of it and even sang one of Dad's old favourites while the iPod played a tune in Dad's pocket.

With the sun behind them and a cool breeze blowing, it really was one of those perfect Dad and Son moments caught in time to save in their memories forever.

Chapter 16

"Two diet cokes please" started Dad.
"Mixed kebab grill, three poppadum, chicken korma, rice, and garlic bread please"

"Perfect" said Eric, "all my favourites."

"Coming right up" said Raj the owner of the restaurant.

Eric put his hand across the table and grabbed Dad's.

Dad gave a smile that Eric hadn't seen in a long while, and yet Eric knew he didn't look or feel well. Dad's eyes had an empty look, and he looked much thinner.

"So" said Dad,

"I've worked out how to do the ultimate never been done before super amazing disappearing magic trick"

He continued, "Looking at the clips you showed me, I can see where others have failed, I have worked out a way of doing it."

Over the next ten minutes, he explained a magical theory of vanishing to Eric.

"But..." Dad continued. He paused for quite a while. In fact, it was a very long while.

"It is a disappearing FOREVER trick, you know what that means?" He emphasised the word FOREVER

Eric didn't speak, but nodded very slowly and squeezed Dad's hand.

Dad carried on, "Do you know what forever means?"

Eric nodded again very slowly.

A realisation of the last few months was starting to come into Eric's mind.

The constant coughing, the sickness, the secret talks late at night, his Aunt coming to stay, all those people coming and going and Dad's new tablets, so many tablets.

And now Dad was going to disappear, forever.

At that point Dad stood up and turned around, spoke to Raj the owner and signalled to Eric that he was going to the toilet.

Raj sat with Eric while he was gone and fiddled with the table settings nervously, moving all the forks around before putting them all back where they started.

In the toilets, Dad fell to his knees on the floor.

No longer could he hold back his tears. Tonight was truth night. Somehow tonight was the night that he had to let Eric know that things were going to change, and soon.

Dad sobbed and sobbed in the toilet, he had started the story that ultimately would lead to Eric having an understanding that Dad wasn't going to be around forever.

Chapter 17

The next morning was a grey day. That's what Eric called days when Dad wasn't well.

He waited outside the bathroom door and listened. Dad was really having a bad day today. He could hear coughing, the odd trump and then Dad having yet another wee.

He also heard the familiar sound of Dad sorting his tablets.

When Dad came out he looked greyer than the sky outside.

"Hey tiny" he whispered to Eric, "what are you waiting around here for?"

"I'm waiting for my Dad" said Eric, giving him a massive smile to cheer him up. It did.

"What are we doing today?" Eric asked, hoping for something happy and fun to be in the answer.

It wasn't going to be fun at all, he knew that by Dad's colouring.

"Well," said Dad "you know what we talked about last night" he gave Eric a slow wink and a nod, "Well I have to go and see someone about..." he paused "...preparation for that.." he paused again "..the magic disappearing trick"

He waited about 5 seconds then continued "I have to go and see a specialist to make sure everything will be ok."

Eric looked back at his Dad. Some of the coded message was getting through to him, but at seven years old some of it was still a bit mysterious. He kind of guessed what he thought he knew, but didn't know everything.

"Ok" said Eric, "what time do we go?"

There was another long pause as Dad rattled his brain for a response, then he said "10.30am, are you coming with me? Great"

And so the day was set, maybe not such a grey day after all. Dad and Son were together again.

No matter what was ahead of them they both knew that time together was so important, and whatever they did they would make it an adventure.

Dad was counting every second of every day. Both he and Mum and the specialist, as Eric knew him now, knew just how quickly the days were counting down.

Chapter 18

The building they were stood outside of was massive, and huge white slabs of walls rose into the sky.

There were signs everywhere and Eric pulled a face that looked like he was trapped in a maze.

"How do we know where to go Dad?" he asked, his head spinning to look in every direction all at once.

"This way sunshine" Dad replied, "Follow the white and green signs. Each department here has its own colour scheme. And mine is white and green"

"Coooool" said Eric.

Inside, the building seemed even bigger, corridors shot off in every direction, and each one was filled with at least one hundred doors, each with names of specialists on written on gold coloured plaques. They made their way to a particular door and entered it.

The waiting room was no bigger than Eric's bedroom.

It was far too small for ten people to sit quietly in without hearing everyone else's conversations.

Eric's ears were running overtime trying to pick up what people were saying.

"Why are all these other people here Dad?" he asked. "Are they here for the same reason you are?"

Dad gulped a massive gulp.

He hadn't thought this through, "What if Eric overhears something about my real reason for the visit to the Hospital?" he thought.

"I think" Dad started "that this is just a waiting room for anyone, maybe even for the canteen" he smiled hoping Eric could be fooled by this.

Eric's eyes darted around the room, every wall had a medical poster, the two tables had Hospital booklets, and the other people waiting, all had paperwork in their hands similar to Dad's.

He looked back at Dad ready to confront him about why they were here again, but then left it and looked at the floor for a while, not forgetting to grab Dad's hand and give it three tight squeezes.

The woman sitting one space away from Eric, whom he had noticed clearly, was reading a booklet titled "DEALING WITH CANCER"

He said nothing, just sat holding Dad's hand and waited, and waited, and waited.

Chapter 19

A very short and round bespectacled man sat at the desk in the room that Eric and Dad had been shown into.

A Toblerone-shaped sign on his desk read Dr Phillip Goldberg.

Dad spoke first, "Good morning Phil, I've brought my son Eric today, he was interested in the preparation for my disappearing trick"

He followed the line with a wink that Eric didn't see and waited with raised eyebrows to check the Doctor had caught on.

After a very short pause, the Doctor nodded at Dad.

"Ok, hello Eric", he said, "we just need to check some of your Dad's blood today, is that ok with you?"

Eric nodded, not having a clue what that meant, it all sounded very exciting he thought.

Ten minutes later they were finished.

Dad's blood had been taken from his arm, a sight that Eric was amazed about, and with the Hospital now behind them, they drove out towards one of their favourite places, the canal.

It was time for lunch and a chat.

"This chat was going to be a tough one" Dad thought.

Chapter 20

"Do you know where magicians go when they disappear?" asked Dad whilst still driving.

There was a long pause from Eric, "Nope, where?"

Dad was about to make up one of the biggest most ridiculous made up stories of his life.

A story that needed telling to his seven-year-old son, because the truth was too much to tell.

The actual truth was too much for either of them to take on.

"Well" said Dad, "There's a magical place, a kingdom in fact, a secretive land that only the chosen amazing magicians and heroes can get to."

Eric sat with his mouth open as Dad described this special place that he would be going to.

Dad went on, "And I won't have that awful cough anymore once I am there, I won't feel any more chest or back pain and maybe, just maybe, my trumps will stop"

He went on "and from where I'm going I can see everything that happens here, I can watch you grow, I can see all your adventures, I can see every game of football you ever play."

Eric giggled, it was only a little laugh because his next question was going to finish Dad off for the rest of the day.

"Why do you have to go? Why can't you stay here with me?" he asked.

Eric didn't look up, he stared at his knees in the car, which was just as well as tears were pouring down Dad's face and his bottom lip was shaking as he bit the inside of his cheeks.

"We can have a chat about that tonight mate" Dad managed to say.

Chapter 21

Eric sat on his bed. Around him were his favourite photos of him and Dad, the camping trip, the walk near the canal, and the holiday last year.

He had a chocolate bar in his hand that had melted onto his fingers. He didn't care. He only had one horrible thought,

''Dad was going''

He didn't really understand how, where or even why but he knew he was losing his Dad and his best friend forever.

No matter what Dad said about a magical kingdom, Eric still knew how much he was going to miss his Dad. He was going to have to grow up without his Dad.

His next thought was ''When? When was Dad going to disappear?''

Chapter 22

Dad sat on the chair near the window, Mum was sat on the sofa and Eric was in between them on the other chair.

Either he'd just been caught stealing sweets and was in for a telling off, or it was time for a serious chat.

Mum and Dad both sipped their tea.

Dad spoke first.

"So Eric, you know I've been a bit poorly? Well, Doctor Gee thinks maybe I should stay at the specialist's centre, see if they can help my cough and my back pains."

Eric just stared at him unable to come up with any words.

Dad continued, "so I have booked myself in to stay there, not here."

Eric's face didn't move a muscle. He just kept looking at Dad wondering how much paler and thinner he would get.

Mum couldn't speak, she just sipped her tea.

"I've agreed to go in next week son, Monday" Dad said with a tight lip. It was obvious he was fighting off tears.

Mum turned her head and promptly left the room. The kitchen door closed behind her.

Dad leant forward, held Eric's hand, winked at him and whispered

"It's time"

Then in a voice that Mum could hear said,

"So, little man, what shall we do over the next few days before I go in?
Fancy a little trip somewhere, just you and me?
A little holiday in the Lake District?"

Chapter 23

Eric and Dad were up at 6 am, an early start to a weekend away, just the two of them.

Dad looked dreadful, however, managed to give a big smile as Eric hugged him like he did every day.

Mum had promised to drive them to the Lakes as Dad felt so tired.

This was going to be a very special weekend. Dad promised "one they would store in the memory bank forever", a phrase he loved to use.

At 7.15 they were packed and ready, the car was warming up and Eric was running around the house getting everything together.

"One more toilet visit" shouted Dad, "you know what I'm like"

And so they were off, it was a two-hour drive so Dad slept to save his energy while Eric looked at the scenery from the back seat.

"Mum" asked Eric, "will Dad be ok this weekend, he seems very tired"

She took a while to answer, but finally commented "your Dad wouldn't miss this no matter what, bear with him, he will do his best"

At the Hotel a young man came out to greet them, he carried the bags which was a big relief for Dad, Mum said her goodbyes and left the two of them to have some fun.

Dad took a selfie outside the Hotel, just him and his boy, Eric.

"I think the sun's coming out Son" said Dad, looking up to the sky, "fancy a trip on that boat over there?" and he pointed to the lakeside boathouse.

"It goes in fifteen minutes, let's do it"

He didn't need an answer from Eric, his face said it all.

Once on the boat, Dad found a comfy seat, leant back against the wall and got his feet up on the chair in front. "Can you let me have fifteen minutes Son? I'm whacked, I promise I'll be right as rain after fifteen minutes"

Eric snuggled up next to his Dad, got comfy with his feet just reaching the chair opposite and promptly closed his eyes too, just happy to be here with him was enough.

He knew this was a special time.

When he woke up Dad was still fast asleep so Eric sneaked the phone from Dad's jacket and grabbed another selfie, this time with Dad's mouth wide open and his tongue half hanging out.

After another five minutes, it was time to wake him, not an easy task these days. Eric knew his Dad had tablets that knocked him out so gave some extra hard prods until Dad came to.

"Ice cream time Dad" said Eric, "can we? please?"

After the boat trip and ice cream, they both had lunch in the Hotel restaurant, what a posh affair that was.

Three sets of knives and forks, the brightest white plates you could have imagined and a waiter all of their own fetching every little need they had.

"It was as if the whole Hotel was there just for himself and Dad", Eric thought.

The rest of their time over the two days was fun filled, in between lots of little rests for Dad.

They played mini golf, snooker, another boat trip that Dad missed completely, a small walk and the best meals out ever, not that Dad ate much.

Dad and Eric talked so much over those two days. Dad talked about his life, how much he enjoyed his time with his kids and Mum, about his family, and made a special point about life and how short it can be.

He told Eric never to put things off, live now, enjoy yourself, don't delay anything.

He also told Eric how proud he was to have him and that since the day he was born he has loved him more and more every second.

Eric told Dad he was his best friend and this made Dad laugh, smile and cry all at once.

Dad took loads of pictures, mostly selfies of the two of them.

Eric had the best weekend ever with Dad, "one for the memory bank" he said to Dad. This was met with a massive smile from an exhausted looking Dad.

On the drive home with Mum, they chatted about Dad's needed trips to the specialist again, and that he was going to go and stay there shortly.

That made Eric look really glum in the back of the car, and as Dad looked forward they both had tears running down their cheeks.

They both knew that this weekend had been special for a reason, Dad was going to be doing his disappearing trick quite soon and it seemed nothing could stop it happening.

"Love you Dad" Eric said from the back of the car.
"Love you more" said Dad,
"Love you mostest" they both replied.

They both had a little smile.

Chapter 24

December 15th

It had been two weeks now since their trip away, and Eric had only seen his Dad three times since he had gone to stay at the specialists.

He missed him massively.

Every school day dragged on, every hour he awaited news that Dad was home again, but at 3.45pm the news didn't come.

The headmaster walked Eric out as his Auntie was picking him up today.

"Is my Dad home?" he asked. She could only shake her head as words didn't come out.

That drive home took forever, Eric was sure they had gone around the same block three times.

Eric looked out through the rear car window. Shoppers were running around collecting Christmas trees and presents and food and treats.

Eric felt nothing. Christmas wasn't for him this year, he only wanted one thing, and sadly that wasn't to be.

They pulled up the driveway at home. The curtains were closed in the front room.

His Auntie had only spoken about three words for the whole journey.

"Let's get in and see your Mum" she said coming round to his side and holding out her gloved hand for his.

In the front room was Gran, Grandad, Eric's big Sister and Uncle Alan, all sat around Mum who looked like she had been crying for hours.

Mum held her arms out straight and Eric ran into them, holding her as tight as possible.

It didn't need to be said but Mum managed to get the words out anyway,

"Your Dad's gone Eric, I'm so sorry" with which she burst into tears and squeezed her son against her even tighter. Everyone in the room was crying.

Eric was crying too.

Chapter 25

Christmas Day

The last ten days were more than likely going to be the building blocks for Eric's future.

He had learned a pain no seven-year-old should ever feel.

He had also grown up so quickly, but also become so lonely, sitting in his room for hours thinking of his Dad.

On one occasion, whilst Eric was upstairs the doorbell had rung, making Eric run down shouting "Is it my Dad?" causing more tears throughout the house.

Of course, it wasn't Dad. Dad had gone.

Today was Christmas day.

It didn't feel like it in the Jones household. Although all the preparations had been taken care of, the tree was up, but no one was in the mood for it.

All the family were in the main lounge, Eric included. The television was off, the main lights were dimmed, outside the sky was black with cloud and no one was speaking.

A turkey sat in the oven, cold. No one had even bothered to turn the heat on.

At 11 am finally his Gran said they should at least open some presents.

"We've paid for them" she said "no point in going to waste."

They took their turns, each receiving a small token from one another, a foul smelling perfume for Gran, socks and a razor for Grandad, some CDs for his Sister and a small red remote control car for Eric.

No one looked too pleased. The usual fun of giving little presents had left them.

By 12 pm there were only three boxes left, his sister got some more hats off Gran, Mum had a small chain and finally there was just one gift left far away at the back of the tree, something that had been overlooked.

Eric leant in to get it, it was a stretch. The gold label was hand written, it said ERIC and it was Dad's handwriting.

Eric stood upright, shocked but excited.

He took a step backwards from the tree, looked around the room at each family member's faces then promptly left the lounge to hide in his bedroom with his gift from Dad.

Chapter 26

"Dearest Eric, my best friend, my super amazing and bestest son" the letter started.

Eric could hear Dad's voice reading it to him.

"I am so sorry that I cannot be with you. I know you will be missing me, and you know I miss you too."

The letter from Dad was wrapped up with another gift. He started opening it immediately whilst carrying on reading.

"I want you to know I am at peace here, I no longer cough, I no longer have any pains, I am no longer on a million tablets and I don't sleep all day.
However, the trumping didn't stop, in fact, because your Mum can't hear me, I trump even more than ever before"

Eric laughed. The letter continued.

"I have been the proudest of Dads the last seven years, watching you grown into a fine young man, I know my timing to leave you was awful, but I also know you have the strength within you to carry on.

I will always be watching over you, I will guide you when I can and give you the strength you need. I will always be close by and always in your heart.

Please remember me for the fun times, the happy days, the trips out, the walks, the talks and the smiles and cuddles.

Live your life to the full Eric, remember don't stress about the small things when you have no idea what's around the corner.

Life is for living today not tomorrow, please don't wait for anything. Do it now. And live to be happy. Don't spend another minute wondering if this or that, just get on and do things.

And most of all be happy for no reason, just choose to be happy, always.

Please take care of your Mum and Sister. You are the man of the house now.

I hope you like the gift I left you, it's my memory bank of all the fun things we have done together."

Eric tore open the rest of the wrapped gift. It was a hard backed book, a big thick one. On the front was the selfie of Eric and Dad outside the Hotel in the Lake District, both smiling.

Across the top of the book was the title:
ME AND MY DAD, THE MAGICIAN

Eric ran his fingers through the pages, it was filled with pictures, selfies mainly, loads of funny one liners, and some terrible jokes from Dad.

It also contained some wise words and advice that all Dads want to share with their Sons, something that should be spread over twenty of thirty years, but this family wasn't to be that lucky.

Eric smiled for the first time in weeks. His little fingers gripped the book tightly as his eyes went back to the letter from Dad.

"I will always love you, Eric. You have been the bestest friend any Dad could have ever wanted. Go out and live your life to the fullest.

Make every day special and do not cry over me anymore, your time is now. Go and have some fun before it's too late

Love you mostest
Dad x"

He stood for two minutes, reading again a few lines from Dad, then folded the letter and placed it into the big book. He pulled it to his chest in a vice like grip, smiled a huge smile and ran downstairs to his family.

His huge smile alone brightened the room. His excitement filled everyone else's faces with joy, as he showed everyone the pages of the book, and he read the letter from Dad to them all.

He repeated the lines that Dad had said to him, and then in a way only the innocence of a child could do he got everybody up on their feet to see Christmas Day through as it should be.

The lights went on, as did the TV, pouring Ant and Dec's Christmas Day show into the room.

On went the oven for Mum, and the radio too filling the kitchen with Christmas cheesy hits from yesteryear.

Gran was given the peeling of potatoes duty, and even the headphone wearing teenager joined in, even if just to ruffle up Eric's hair.

"Everything is going to be Ok" proclaimed Eric. "Life will go on and it will be fab"

As the family joyfully got on with Christmas, as did the rest of the world, Eric looked up and out into the sky from the large lounge bay window.

"Love you Dad" he whispered to himself quietly, and he knew Dad was replying in the most magical of ways as he finished his words the very first pure white snowflake fell down right in front of him, followed by a billion more.

Eric shouted his family who all came to look out at the now steady stream of snow turning the outside world a beautiful shade of white.

Mum stood close behind Eric put her hands on his shoulders, leant down and whispered to him,

"That'll be your magic Dad who did this"

The End

18029946R00044

Printed in Poland
by Amazon Fulfillment
Poland Sp. z o.o., Wrocław